Buon Appetito!

— AnBal.

Rosie's Red Sauce

This Book Belongs to

_____

_____

_____

Rosie's Red Sauce

Written by Armand Buzzelli
Illustrated by Amanda Beuchat

Buzzelli, Armand.
Rosie's Red Sauce
1. Children   2. Ethnicity   3. Cooking   4. Family
ISBN 9781735733135
Illustrations by Amanda Beuchat

First Paperback Edition

Leo & Maya,

May you make your own sauce.

- A.B.

Rosie and Grandpa
skip along the street,
swinging to the market
to find a tasty treat.

"No, we don't want cake
and we don't want pie.
Our favorite red sauce
is all we want to buy!"

"Yum, yummy red sauce,
it fills up our bellies.
Let's buy a great big jar
of sauce over at the deli."

The store fills with smells of bread, pie, and cakes.
A baker casts a smile, while fresh biscotti bakes.

Rosie jumps and laughs
once she sees the prize;
a sea of red sauce jars
right before her very eyes.

Grandpa reaches way up
to the top shelf.
Grabs a jar of red sauce
as he hums to himself.

"No, we don't want cake
and we don't want pie.
Our favorite red sauce
is all we want to buy!"

"Yum, yummy red sauce,
it fills up our bellies.
Let's buy a great big jar
of sauce over at the deli!"

Back at Grandpa's house,
music fills the air.
A pot of sauce bubbles.
Rosie smiles from her chair.

They sing and they eat,
a feast for the books.
Rosie loves her Grandpa
and all the food he cooks.

One sunny morning,
on Grandpa's birthday,
Rosie skips to the store,
her feet know the way.

"Grandpa won't want cake.
He never eats pie.
Our favorite red sauce
is all I need to buy!"

"Yum, yummy red sauce,
it fills up our bellies.
I'll buy a great big jar of
sauce over at the deli!"

Rosie sees the store
and stops right in her tracks.
She peeps a sign on the door:
"DELI CLOSED. PLEASE COME BACK!"

Rosie's shoulders slump
and her eyes fill with tears.
She'd planned to make a meal
to honor Grandpa's years.

"No red sauce, no 'yum!'
Dinner's down the drain.
Grandpa's birthday is wrecked!"
... Then it began to rain.

Rosie shivers and shakes.
She's soaked to the core.
Trudging back down the lane
she sees Grandpa's front door.

"Get out of the rain, dear."
Grandpa hugs her back.
"The store was closed, Grandpa!"
Her voice starts to crack.

Back in the warm house,
Rosie spies through glass.
She spots red tomatoes
growing up from the grass.

"Grandpa, our red sauce…
why's it the best in town?"
"Fresh veggies, tomatoes,
and a cook who slows down."

"Grandpa! Your garden!
Let's use it for sauce!
Let's start picking veggies!
Our day won't be a loss!"

Rosie and Grandpa
pick, and pick, and pick.
They laugh and sing loudly.
"This party is perfect!"

They cut and they stir
and they mix, mix, mix.
Rosie takes a spoonful
and thinks that she's been tricked!

"Wow, Grandpa!" she screams,
"It's tasty and sweet!
It's better than the store;
the best you'll ever eat!"

"Rosie, here is something
you should be proud of…
everything tastes better
when you make it with love."

After her red sauce,
Rosie cooks more things.
And she and her Grandpa
always make time to sing:

"No, we don't want pie
and we don't want cake.
Our favorite red sauce
is all we want to make!"

"Yum, yummy red sauce,
it fills up our bellies.
Let's make a great big jar of
sauce *better* than the deli!"

The End.

Recipe for Rosie's Red Sauce
(Recipe makes approximately 5 cups of marinara sauce)

Ingredients
- 1/3 cup extra virgin olive oil
- 2 cloves of garlic (slice into thin pieces)
- Salt and freshly ground pepper, to taste
- Two 28-ounce cans peeled, crushed plum tomatoes or 10 to 12 whole peeled tomatoes
- 10 basil leaves, chopped, or 1 tablespoon dried
- 1 tablespoon chopped parsley, or 1 teaspoon dried

Directions
In a medium sauce pan over medium-low heat, heat the oil. Sauté the garlic, salt, and pepper for 5 minutes or until garlic is softened. Add remaining ingredients, then raise the heat to medium-high and bring to a simmer, stirring often. Simmer for 30 minutes.

About Us

Author - Armand Buzzelli
Dr. Armand Buzzelli works in student affairs at Robert Morris University in Pittsburgh, PA. As a proud father of two young children, he loves to teach lessons through storytelling. Armand hopes to encourage children to embrace their personal heritage through traditions such as cooking together. Armand enjoys sports, being with his family, and of course…. good red sauce.

"It can be difficult to properly explain the importance of healthy home cooking and family traditions to your children. Rosie's Red Sauce promotes those values and serves as a model for families that want to plant their own gardens and make time to cook together. This is also a love story to grandparents and the important role they play in shaping the lives of their grandchildren."
- Armand Buzzelli, Ph.D.

Illustrator – Amanda Beuchat
Amanda is a senior at Robert Morris University, pursuing her BFA in Media Arts with a concentration in Graphic Design. She enjoys drawing, photography and watching Pittsburgh sports. She resides with her family in the suburbs of Pittsburgh.

Made in the USA
Middletown, DE
01 November 2020